MR. IMPOSSIBLE

by Roger Hargreaves

WORLD INTERNATIONAL

Mr Impossible could do the most amazing things.

For instance, Mr Impossible could jump over a house.

You try it.

It's impossible!

And Mr Impossible could make himself invisible.

All he had to do was stand there and think about becoming invisible, and he became invisible.

You try it.

It's impossible!

And Mr Impossible could fly.

All he had to do was stand there and flap his arms about, and off he flew.

You try it.

It's impossible!

And, Mr Impossible lived in an impossible looking house.

Have you ever seen a house in such an impossible place?

Of course not!

One day Mr Impossible was out walking in the woods, when he met a boy called William.

William was on his way to school.

"Hello," said Mr Impossible.

"Hello," replied William. "I'm William."

"I'm Impossible," said Mr Impossible.

"Really?" said William.

"Really," smiled Mr Impossible.

"Can you do impossible things?" asked William.

"Haven't come across anything I couldn't do," replied Mr Impossible, modestly.

William thought.

"Can you climb up that tree?" he asked, pointing to the biggest tree in the wood.

"I can do better than that," replied Mr Impossible. "I can walk up that tree!"

And he did!

William thought again.

"Can you stand on one hand?" he asked.

"I can do better than that," replied Mr Impossible. "I can stand on no hands!"

And he did!

"That's impossible," cried William.

"True," replied Mr Impossible.

Then William remembered that he was on his way to school.

"Why don't you come with me?" he asked.

"But I've never been to a school before," Mr Impossible said.

"Then it's time you did," replied William. "Come on!"

William and Mr Impossible sat at the back of William's classroom with all the other children.

The teacher came in, but didn't notice that there was somebody extra in his class that morning.

"Good morning, children," said the teacher. "I have a very difficult sum for you to do today. It will take you most of the morning to work out the answer."

And he wrote the sum on the blackboard.

It really was the most difficult sum William had ever seen in his whole life. Full of multiplications and divisions and additions and other things William didn't enjoy.

The teacher was right. It would indeed take most of the morning to work out the answer, if not most of the afternoon as well.

Mr Impossible whispered in William's ear.

William put up his hand.

"Yes, William," said the teacher. "Is there something about the sum you don't understand?"

"Please, sir," said William. "Is the answer 23?"

The teacher was very, absolutely, totally, completely amazed.

"How did you work out the sum so quickly?" he gasped. "It's impossible!"

"Nothing is impossible," said Mr Impossible from the back of the class, and stood up.

"Well I never did," exclaimed the teacher.

After that, Mr Impossible spent all day at the school.

He showed the teacher how he could read a book upside down.

"That's impossible," said the children who were watching.

"Absolutely," replied Mr Impossible.

Then William asked Mr Impossible if he would like to play in the school football match.

"Oo, yes please," replied Mr Impossible. "I've never played football before."

And do you know what he did?

He kicked the football so high into the air that when it came down, it had snow on it!

What an impossible thing to do!

Then it was time to go home.

Mr Impossible said goodbye to all the people at the school, and then said goodbye to William.

"Goodbye, Mr Impossible," said William.

"Goodbye, William," said Mr Impossible, and just disappeared.

William rubbed his eyes, and went home.

William's mother and father were waiting for him.

"Hello, William," they said. "Did you have a good day at school?"

"Yes," replied William. "And I met somebody who can do anything in the world!"

"Really William," they both laughed. "You're impossible!"

William smiled, and went inside.

And, a hundred miles away, a small figure was listening to what William's mother and father were saying.

And he grinned an impossible grin, and then he went to sleep.

Standing on his head!

And we all know, that's . . .

. . . Impossible!

MORE SPECIAL OFFERS
FOR MR MEN AND LITTLE MISS READERS

In every Mr Men and Little Miss book like this one, and now in the Mr Men
sticker and activity books, you will find a special token. Collect six tokens and we
will send you a gift of your choice.

Choose either a Mr Men or Little Miss poster, or a Mr Men or Little Miss
double sided full colour bedroom door hanger.

Return this page with six tokens per gift required to
Marketing Dept., MM / LM Gifts, World International Ltd., Deanway Technology Centre,
Wilmslow Road, Handforth, Cheshire SK9 3FB

|--- 100 mm ---|

Your name:_____ Age: ____

Address: _____

_____Postcode: _____

Parent / Guardian Name (Please Print) _____

Please tape a 20p coin to your request to cover part post and package cost

I enclose six tokens per gift, please send me:-

Posters:-   Mr Men Poster ☐   Little Miss Poster ☐

Door Hangers - Mr Nosey / Muddle ☐   Mr Greedy / Lazy ☐

            Mr Tickle / Grumpy ☐   Mr Slow / Quiet ☐

            Mr Messy / Noisy ☐

            L Miss Fun / Late ☐   L Miss Helpful / Tidy ☐

            L Miss Busy / Brainy ☐   L Miss Star / Fun ☐

Please Tick Appropriate Box

ENTRANCE FEE SAUSAGES

250 mm

MR. GREEDY

Collect six of these tokens
You will find one inside every
Mr Men and Little Miss book
which has this special offer.

1 TOKEN

We may occasionally wish to advise you of other Mr Men gifts.
If you would rather we didn't please tick this box ☐

Offer open to residents of UK, Channel Isles and Ireland only

Join the

MR. MEN & little miss
Club

Treat your child to membership of the popular Mr Men & Little Miss Club and see their delight when they receive a personal letter from Mr Happy and Little Miss Giggles, a club badge with their name on, and a superb Welcome Pack. And imagine how thrilled they'll be to receive a birthday card and Christmas card from the Mr Men and Little Misses!

Take a look at all of the great things in the Welcome Pack,

 every one of them of superb quality (see box right). If it were on sale in the shops, the Pack alone would cost around £12.00. But a year's membership, including all of the other Club benefits, costs just £8.99 (plus 70p postage) with a 14 day money-back guarantee if you're not delighted.

To enrol your child please send your name, address and telephone number together with your child's full name, date of birth and address (including postcode) and a cheque or postal order for £9.69 (payable to Mr Men & Little Miss Club) to: Mr Happy, Happyland (Dept. WI), PO Box 142, Horsham RH13 5FJ. Or call 01403 242727 to pay by credit card.

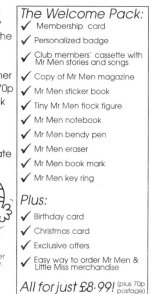

The Welcome Pack:

✓ Membership card
✓ Personalized badge
✓ Club members' cassette with Mr Men stories and songs
✓ Copy of Mr Men magazine
✓ Mr Men sticker book
✓ Tiny Mr Men flock figure
✓ Mr Men notebook
✓ Mr Men bendy pen
✓ Mr Men eraser
✓ Mr Men book mark
✓ Mr Men key ring

Plus:

✓ Birthday card
✓ Christmas card
✓ Exclusive offers
✓ Easy way to order Mr Men & Little Miss merchandise

All for just £8.99! (plus 70p postage)